To Sarah,
with best wishes

Ann Ferns

MUNGO

the mud monster

written by Ann Ferns
illustrated by Susanne Ferrier

lansdowne
sydney · london · auckland · new york

Not many people know about
the Mud Age. Mention the
Ice Age, or the Bronze Age to
almost anyone and they will
nod very knowingly and say,
'Ah yes, of course.' Extra
clever people might even
be able to give the dates.
But ask about the Mud Age
and it's a different story.
Even schoolteachers, prime
ministers and other people
who are supposed to know
everything will look blank,
scratch their heads and ask,
'The *what* Age?'

The Mud Age slipped in very
quietly just before the Ice Age.
Because it didn't last very long –
no more than a million years or so
– hardly anyone noticed it. As you
may have guessed, during the Mud Age
the earth was covered with thick, warm,
slurpy mud. It was an age of squelching and
schlooping and squishing and sloshing, when
mud-dwelling monsters, large and small, were the
only creatures one was likely to meet.

Some of the monsters were gruesome and ferocious,
others were not. It all depended on the way they had been

brought up. They paddled through the mud on big, rubbery feet and burbled with joy as it slithered between their toes.

Sometimes they lay down and rolled in it, which was perfectly all right in those days, because soap hadn't been invented and no one worried about getting dirty. The bravest of the monsters would even hold their noses, dive to the bottom of the mud and blow thick, fat, ploppy bubbles.

There was one monster who was not at all ferocious. His name was Mungo and he had never frightened anybody in his life. When he was very young he tried once or twice, just to see what it was like. But Mungo simply didn't have a frightening face. The monsters he tried to scare either laughed very loudly, or put their noses in the air and pretended he wasn't there.

Nor was Mungo very brave. Only once did he dive down to the bottom of the mud. It took him three days to work up enough courage to do it, and when he got down there everything was so black and crawly that he had bad dreams about it for a week. So he didn't do it again.

Apart from monsters, the only other creature that lived in the Mud Age was the Drongo bird. It was a very rare bird indeed; so rare that there was actually only one. She was rather bossy and liked to have her own way, and the monsters didn't like her very much. Because she wasn't a beautiful bird, she tried to make herself more interesting by wearing large hats, which she made herself. But the only one who found her interesting was Mungo.

He thought that she was probably lonely, being the only Drongo bird in the world. So he always did his best to be friendly, and admired her hats even when he thought they were terrible.

One day Mungo was just slopping along and enjoying the 'sloink' that his feet made every time he pulled them out of the mud, when he came across Drongo bird very hard at work. She was weaving reeds and branches together into a large circle.

'What a magnificent hat,' said Mungo. 'You'll look very smart in that.'

'It's not a hat,' snapped Drongo bird. 'It's a nest.'

'I see,' said Mungo. Then he asked, 'Where will you wear it?'

Drongo bird gave a sigh. 'I shall not wear it,' she explained very carefully. 'I shall live in it.'

'Oh,' said Mungo because he couldn't think of anything else to say.

Soon a group of monsters had gathered to watch the building of the nest. They sneered and giggled and made rude remarks.

None of this seemed to worry Drongo bird at all. But Mungo blushed bright pink with embarrassment for her.

'I'll help you if you like,' he offered, glaring at the bad-mannered monsters.

So all afternoon Mungo and Drongo bird wove the reeds and branches together and slapped mud over the top until they had built something magnificent. Mungo didn't know what a nest was supposed to look like, so he wasn't sure if they had it right. But Drongo bird seemed very pleased with it.

All the other monsters had grown bored and sploshed away to do something else. Evening was coming and the sky had turned to a cold purple-grey. A bleak wind moaned and muttered across the great mudlands and Mungo shivered.

'Come along,' squawked Drongo bird. 'Let's go inside.'

Mungo looked at the nest. 'What? In there?' he asked.

'Of course,' said Drongo bird impatiently. 'What do you think we built it for?'

Mungo had been hoping that she wouldn't ask him that, because he had no idea. He was very relieved when she answered the question herself.

'It's to keep us snug and warm. There's cold weather in the air.'

This was one of the times when Mungo wished that he was just slightly brave. He really didn't want to go into the nest, because he was afraid that it would be like diving to the bottom of the mud – very dark and creepy. But he didn't want to hurt Drongo bird's feelings either, so he closed his eyes and took a deep breath and crawled inside.

When he opened his eyes again he found that everything was much better than he'd expected. The nest *was* dark, but it had a nice smell of wood and leaves and dried mud. The wind was snarling and growling and throwing itself at the walls, but it couldn't get inside.

'Move over!' ordered Drongo bird, squeezing herself in after Mungo and pulling some branches across the doorway. 'There's plenty of room for both of us.'

That wasn't quite true. In fact, they were extremely squashed, but Mungo didn't complain. Drongo bird's feathers were soft and warm and to curl up close beside her gave him a cosy, snoozy, drowsy feeling. Drongo bird tucked her wing over Mungo's head and snug, dry and safe from the weather, they both fell asleep.

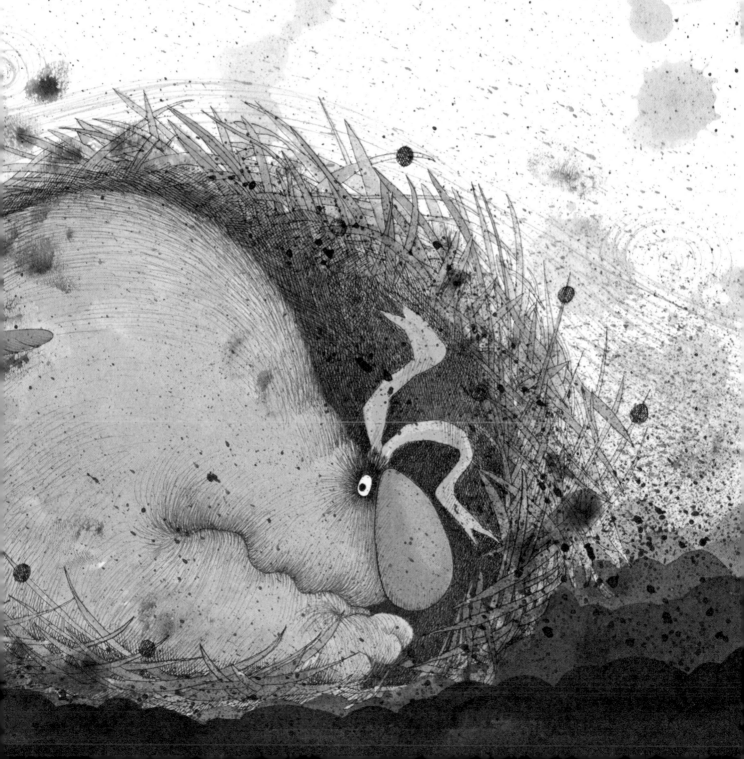

Outside the night grew colder and colder, for the Mud Age was
almost over and the Ice Age was about to begin. First a crisp,
crackling frost came creeping across the land and turned the mud
to crystal. Then a flurry and flutter of snowflakes swished softly and
silently down from the sky. It snowed and snowed and froze and
froze. Slowly, everything disappeared under shimmering, sparkling
sheets of ice. There was no more mud, no more monsters, nothing
but snowdrifts and icebergs and great glistening glaciers.

Deep under the snow, Mungo and Drongo bird slept on in their
nest. They didn't hear the Ice Age arrive and they didn't hear it
leave. The sun came out and the earth grew warm again. A million
years of history came and went, but nothing disturbed their
comfortable dreams.

PROF. P. PLATT

B.A. (HONS), Th.L,
Bsc., B.C.L., B.D.S.
G.P., Ph.D, PhL.

Somehow, after all that time, the Mud Age got left out of the history books and very few people knew that it had existed. There was one man, however, who had a very shrewd idea that there must have once been a Mud Age. His name was Professor Percival Platt.

He lived in a large house with a sign on the door that read:
Prof. P. Platt B.A. (Hons), Th.L., Bsc., B.C.L., B.D.S., G.P., Phd, PhL. Professor Platt had all these letters after his name because he was very good at passing exams. The PhL at the end of the list stood for Prehistoric Languages. The professor was interested in all things prehistoric, but he couldn't find anyone who could teach him prehistoric languages, so he taught them to himself. He even set himself a prehistoric languages exam, and, of course, passed with flying colours.

Because he couldn't find anything about the Mud Age in books, Professor Platt decided to go out and look for clues himself. He was quite sure that somewhere he would find some signs of that long-ago age. So one day he packed himself some banana sandwiches and a flask of milky tea and set off in his car to look for anything that might have been left over from the Mud Age. The most sensible place to go to was a muddy place. Professor Platt was a very sensible man, so he drove his car to a swamp which was not too far from where he lived.

It was a good day for visiting a swamp, very warm and sticky, with a little light rain to make it extra swampy. The professor parked his car on the grass and took off his shoes and socks. He rolled his trousers up above his knees, and grasping a large walking stick, he waded into the mud. Soft and squishy, it squibbed between his toes and wrapped itself around his ankles. But unlike the monsters of long ago, Professor Platt didn't enjoy the feeling. He muttered 'Urk!' and 'Ughh!' and 'Yuk!' to himself as he squelched along and poked his stick among the reeds.

Just as he was beginning to wish that he'd stayed home and watched television, something very exciting happened. Professor Platt prodded his stick into an extra thick clump of weeds, and someone grunted, 'Umph!'

He prodded again, and someone else squawked, 'Aarkk!'

The long sleep of Mungo and Drongo bird was over. Professor Platt had jabbed his stick right through the door of their nest. The first jab landed on Mungo's furry bottom and the second jab almost knocked Drongo bird's hat off.

Blinking and yawning and grumbling, they slowly crawled out of the nest. There before them was a monster the like of which they'd never seen before. It had a pink face with bushy grey hair at the top and bottom and bright blue eyes that flashed and popped.

'Aha! I knew it!' cried the monster. Neither of them knew what that meant, but when the monster spoke again it was in their own language. 'I am Professor Percival Platt,' he said, in perfect prehistoric. 'And you, I know, are Mud Age Monsters.'

'Wrong!' snapped Drongo bird. 'He's a monster, but I'm a bird.'

'Of course! Of course!' said Professor Platt in great excitement. 'The Drongo bird. You've been extinct for a million years.'

'I have *not*,' said Drongo bird. 'I've been asleep.'

Mungo wished she wouldn't keep arguing with the professor. He was only small, but he did have that big stick, and he seemed like someone who should be treated with respect.

'You must come home with me,' insisted Professor Platt. 'I have to find out all about you.'

'All right,' said Mungo.

Professor Platt waved his stick. 'You'll be famous!' he cried. 'Wonders of the World!'

'Oh well, that's different.' Drongo bird had always wanted to be a Wonder of the World. She straightened her hat and fluffed up her feathers.

'Please lead the way, dear professor,' she beamed.

They slurped across the swamp and clambered up the bank to where the car was waiting.

Professor Platt took some old sheets out of the boot and spread them on the seats.

'Mud isn't good for cars,' he explained.

'Is this where you live?' asked Mungo, wondering how they would all fit into the professor's nest.

Professor Platt laughed so much that Mungo knew he'd made a good joke. He hoped that he could remember it to tell another time.

Somehow, the professor managed to get them both into the car. Drongo bird insisted on having the back seat to herself, which meant that Mungo had to squeeze into the front with the professor. This took a great deal of pushing and huffing, and even when most of Mungo was inside the car, parts of him overflowed. But it was the best they could do.

What happened next was the most terrifying thing in Mungo's whole life. It was worse than being jumped on by the fiercest of ferocious monsters. The car gave a sudden wild roar and began to move forward. Rumbling angrily it ran faster and faster, not seeming to care that it was taking Mungo and the professor and Drongo bird with it.

Mungo realised that he had woken up into a strange new world. In the Mud Age there had been only a few trees and bushes, and they were there for nibbling on. But now they were everywhere, covering all the land that had once been a beautiful sea of mud. The main inhabitants of this new world seemed to be cars. They were all colours and shapes and sizes, and, as far as he could make out, their life seemed to be one long race along a track between the trees. They didn't seem to be enjoying the race at all; in fact, it made them very angry. They snarled loudly the whole time, and yelled 'Vroom!' and 'Yaaah!' and other rude things each time they passed one another.

By the time they arrived at the professor's house Mungo was shaking all over. He didn't care what happened to him any more. He didn't even care whether or not they'd won the race. All that mattered was that the car had stopped and he could get out.

On wobbly legs he followed Professor Platt into the house. Drongo bird came up behind, trying to look very cool and calm. But Mungo noticed that her tail feathers were sticking up and her hat was on back to front.

'Right,' said the professor, leading them into his office. 'First of all we're going to have some tests.'

Mungo hoped that tests were something he could eat. He hadn't had anything for a million years, and his stomach was beginning to rumble hungrily.

Professor Platt picked up a notebook and pen from his desk.

'I want to find out how clever you are,' he said.

Drongo bird gave a delighted smile and smoothed her feathers. All her life she'd been trying to tell people how clever she was, and here at last was someone who really wanted to know.

'I make all my own hats,' she said. 'And I designed and built my own nest.'

Mungo tried very hard to think of something clever that he had done, but nothing came to mind.

'What is nine times seven?' asked Professor Platt.

There was a long silence. Then Mungo said helpfully, 'It's quite a lot.'

'Nine times seven *whats*?' Drongo bird wanted to know.

The professor sighed and wrote something in his notebook. 'You're obviously not very clever,' he said. Then he added more cheerfully, 'But not everyone is. Perhaps you're good at sport.'

From out of his cupboard he took a large ball.

'Catch!' he shouted to Drongo bird and threw the ball right at her.

Drongo bird gave a screech and flapped her wings. Flying was not one of the things she did well, but she managed to get out of the way of the ball before she crashed onto the carpet. The ball bounced off Mungo's stomach and he gave a loud 'humph!' and rolled over backwards.

'No sport,' wrote Professor Platt.

'Never mind,' he said, 'tomorrow we'll have tests in art and music and science.'

Mungo didn't know what any of those things were, but he had a feeling he wasn't very good at them.

'Come with me,' said Professor Platt, 'and I'll show you where you're to stay.'

He took them through the house and out into the back yard. When he wasn't taking exams or studying prehistoric times, the professor enjoyed a little gardening. He was very proud of his flower beds and shrubs and his big green lawn with a lily pond in the middle.

'Please make yourselves at home,' he said. Then he went back inside to cook dinner. He wasn't sure what Mud Age creatures liked to eat, but he was certain he could find something in his larder that would take their fancy.

Mungo looked at the sweet, juicy greenery all around them and his stomach rumbled louder than ever.

'Do you think the professor would mind,' he asked, 'if we just had a little nibble?'

'Of course not,' said Drongo bird. 'He said we were to make ourselves at home. And if we were at home it would be dinner time and we would eat.'

The best thing about having Drongo bird for a friend was that she was always right. Happily they munched and chewed and chomped at the garden until neither of them had room for another leaf or blossom.

'Superb!' said Drongo bird, daintily wiping her beak with the tip of her wing. 'Quite the best meal I've ever had.'

Mungo sat down on the grass and thought very hard.

'Drongo,' he said at last, 'when the professor said, "Make yourselves at home", did he mean that we could really make this like home?'

Drongo bird looked at him.

'Are you thinking what I'm thinking?' she asked.

'Yes,' said Mungo. 'I think I am.'

Drongo bird took off her hat and turned it upside down. With both paws, Mungo scooped up soil from the flower bed and dropped it into the hat. When the hat was full, he carried it over to the lily pond and tipped it into the water. Then he went back to the flower bed and filled up the hat again.

It took quite a long time to turn the lily pond into a swamp. But when they had finished, it was so beautifully thick and burbly and oozy that it was worth every minute they'd spent on it.

Drongo bird stepped gracefully into the mud and wriggled around to make herself comfortable. Then she spread her wings and rolled over, her feet in the air, gently wallowing on her back.

Mungo jumped in with a mighty 'sploink' and squirmed joyfully as the soft, warm glug wrapped itself around him.

This really was home.

Professor Platt came out of the house carrying two buckets of porridge. He looked at his bare trees, his chewed-up bushes and his headless flowers, and his mouth fell open. Then he looked at his lily pond and his beard stood on end. His pink face turned to purple and he began to yell. He was so upset that he forgot to yell in prehistoric, but even though Mungo and Drongo bird couldn't understand him, they could tell he wasn't pleased.

'Inside, both of you!' he shouted. 'Into the bath and then to bed. I'll deal with you in the morning!'

Mungo didn't know what a bath was, and when he found out he didn't like it. The water was too hot, the soap went in his eyes, and when Professor Platt scrubbed behind his ears it really hurt. But the worst thing of all was what happened to Drongo bird. Wet and bedraggled, her feathers hanging limp, she burst into tears.

'I want to go home!' she sobbed. 'I want to go ho-o-ome!'

'You can't go home,' said Professor Platt. 'Tomorrow we're going to have more tests. I've telephoned the newspapers and the radio and television and they're all coming to watch. Don't you want to be Wonders of the World?'

Mungo stood up in the bath and shook himself hard. Sprays of water flew all over the room, but he didn't care.

'No!' he said loudly , 'I don't want to be a Wonder of the World!
I don't like nine times seven and I don't like being hit in the stomach
by a ball. I don't like porridge and I don't like baths. I'm *me*.
I'm Mungo! I live in a swamp, I eat leaves and flowers and I love to
cover myself in mud. That's me, and I like being me!'

'Bravo,' sniffled Drongo bird. 'You tell him, Mungo.'

Professor Platt put down the soap and scrubbing brush and looked
up at Mungo.

'My dear fellow,' he said quietly, 'how right you are. Please
forgive me.'

From a rail on the back of the door he took a large, fluffy towel.
'If you'd like to dry yourselves, I'll go and start the car.'

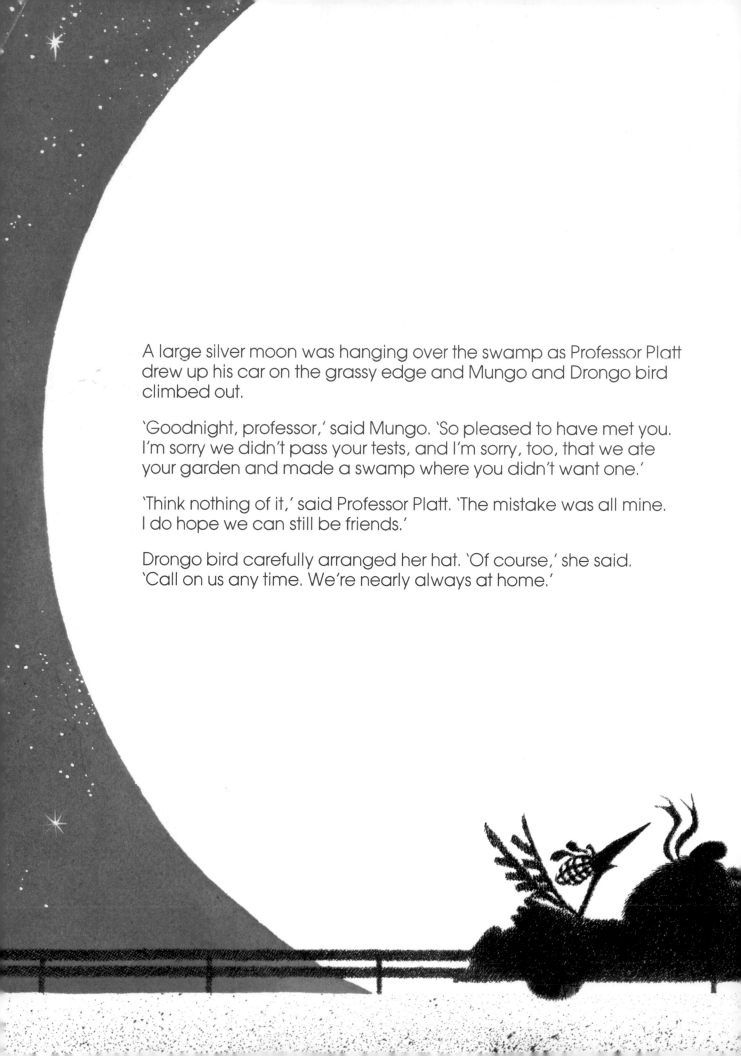

A large silver moon was hanging over the swamp as Professor Platt drew up his car on the grassy edge and Mungo and Drongo bird climbed out.

'Goodnight, professor,' said Mungo. 'So pleased to have met you. I'm sorry we didn't pass your tests, and I'm sorry, too, that we ate your garden and made a swamp where you didn't want one.'

'Think nothing of it,' said Professor Platt. 'The mistake was all mine. I do hope we can still be friends.'

Drongo bird carefully arranged her hat. 'Of course,' she said. 'Call on us any time. We're nearly always at home.'

Together, Mungo and Drongo bird walked down into the mud. Side by side they slurched across to the large clump of reeds where their nest lay hidden. Everything was just as they had left it, warm and snug and very peaceful.

'Mungo,'' yawned Drongo bird, spreading her wing comfortably over him. 'What *is* nine times seven?'

'Don't know,' murmured Mungo drowsily. 'Don't suppose it really matters.'

Published by Lansdowne, Sydney
a division of RPLA Pty Limited
176 South Creek Road, Dee Why West, N.S.W., Australia, 2099.
First published 1984
Text © Ann Ferns 1984
Illustrations © Susanne Ferrier 1984
Produced in Australia by the Publisher
Typeset in Australia by Walter Deblaere & Associates
Printed in Hong Kong by Dai Nippon Printing Co. (HK) Ltd

National Library of Australia Cataloguing-in-Publication Data

Ferns, Ann, 1942–
    Mungo, the mud monster.

    For children.
    ISBN 0 7018 1793 3.
    I. Ferrier, Susanne.   II. Title.

A823'.3

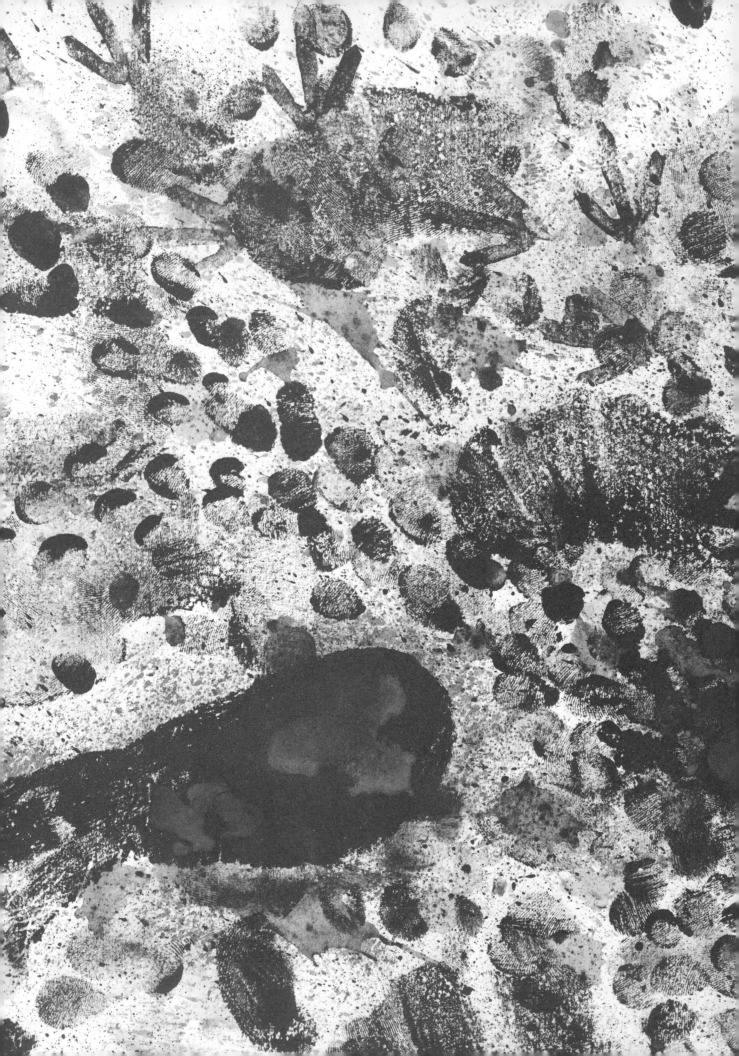